THE DARING PRINCE DASHING

WRITTEN BY
MARILOU T. REEDER

ILLUSTRATED BY
KARL WEST

Sky Pony Press
NEW YORK

For Sophia, Sasha & Annabel—MR
For Kate, Kaitlyn & Ethan—KW

Sky Pony Press books may be purchased in bulk at special discounts for sales promotion, corporate gifts, fund-raising, or educational purposes. Special editions can also be created to specifications. For details, contact the Special Sales Department, Sky Pony Press, 307 West 36th Street, 11th Floor, New York, NY 10018 or info@skyhorsepublishing.com.

Sky Pony is a registered trademark of Skyhorse Publishing, Inc. , a Delaware corporation.

Visit our website at www.skyponypress.com.

10 9 8 7 6 5 4 3 2 1

Manufactured in China, June 2015
This product conforms to CPSIA 2008

Library of Congress Cataloging-in-Publication Data is available on file.

Cover design by Sarah Brody
Cover illustration credit Karl West

Print ISBN: 978-1-63450-161-3
Ebook ISBN: 978-1-63450-926-8

Prince Dashing was daring.

He bathed in the moat with crocodiles.

He dangled upside down from the
tallest tree while eating his snack.

He toasted s'mores by dragon's breath,

and he catapulted himself across the Royal Gardens to mount his stallion.

"Away, Rover!"

The entire kingdom looked on in horror,
especially the king and queen.

The night of the royal ice cream social, children from near and far gathered at the palace. All heads turned when a loud *ZING-BOING! ZING-BOING! ZING-BOING!* came from the entrance.

A mysterious girl walked in.

"What was that peculiar noise?" asked the prince. "This!" said the girl.

"Let me see it," said the prince. But the girl bounded to the tightrope to enjoy her sundae.
The prince liked her instantly.

When Dashing threw sprinkles like confetti to catch them on his tongue, the girl teetered a tower of waffle cones on the tip of her nose.

When he roller-bladed across the grand piano, she did a backbend and played *Für Elise* with her toes.

But at the stroke of bedtime, the girl hurried off.
The prince noticed she'd left something behind.

The next morning after a breakfast of rattlesnake eggs with Whoopin' Hot Sauce, Prince Dashing made an announcement:

"The girl who can make the right sound with this stick-thingy will be an honored guest at my birthday party. I shall roam the kingdom to find her ..."

"Awwwww," said the crowd.

"...while blindfolded!"

"Sheesh," groaned the king.

The queen choked on her bacon.

The townsfolk shook their heads.

and sprinted through forests . . .

"Oops. Pardon me."

until eventually he tripped
into the zoo.

Before the king and queen could catch
him, he scaled a wall and landed at
the feet of a lion.

"Does this belong to you, Miss?"
he asked, accidentally poking the lion's nose.

ROAROO, ROAROOO!

"That doesn't sound right," Prince Dashing said.

Circus

He vaulted over a guardrail and cartwheeled into a hippo.

WHACK! WHOMP! WHACK!...

"That's not right, either," said the prince.

Meanwhile . . .

FOUND
Stick-thingy

Left at Royal Ice
Cream Social

Please call:
1-800-DASHING

The girl wanted her stick back.

When she arrived at the zoo, the gorilla
was going bananas.

The girl sailed through the air . . .

and snatched the stick.

ZING-BOING

ZING-BOING

"That's the sound!" said Prince Dashing.

"Want to come to my royal birthday party next week?"

"No way!" said the girl.

"That is, unless you'll have a zip line."

Prince Dashing thought that was an excellent idea.

And so began a most
adventurous friendship.